FAVORITE PART OF MY DAY!

Written by Nicole Knudtson
Illustrated by Katherine Lenius

favoritepartofday.com

To Greg, Cassidy, and Samantha. Life moves so fast.
I am thankful for each night we slow down to share.
Hearing your favorite part of day always makes me
smile.
- *N.K.*

To Chris, Maddie, Olivia, and Ben. You're always the
favorite part of my day.
- *K.L.*

With the sun
going down and
my friends
in my bed

My teeth are clean

and my book is read

Bedtime continues
when we each
get to say . . .

This was the

FAVORITE PART OF MY DAY!

From the very end

back to the start

Think about your day . . .

what was your favorite part?

Some days it's tough

Some days I have three

Just thinking
of them

fills me
with glee!

We talk about our days for awhile

Then after hugs and kisses

I close my eyes
with a smile

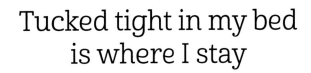

Tucked tight in my bed
is where I stay

Dreaming about tomorrow's . . .

FAVORITE PART of my DAY!

good night

About the Author

Nicole Knudtson

Nicole only dreamt of being able to publish and share this book she wrote years ago. She lives in a suburb of Minneapolis with her husband and two daughters and works full-time at RSM US LLP.

About the Illustrator

Katherine Lenius

Katherine grew up drawing on the walls and now she gets to draw for a living. She lives in a suburb of Minneapolis with her husband and three children where she works as an illustrator and designer.
katherinelenius.com

The author and illustrator met in the third grade and have been friends ever since.

33691422R00019